Atheneum Books for Young Readers
An imprint of Simon & Schuster Children's Publishing Division
1230 Avenue of the Americas
New York, New York 10020
Copyright © 2001 by Paul Goble
Photographs courtesy of Paul Goble
The spirit figures on the endpapers are from Blackfoot tipi covers,
depicting the sources of their power: vital track, kidneys, joints, brain, etc.
Book design by Paul Goble
The text is set in 18 point Monotype Times New Roman.
These pages are printed the same size as the original artwork, which is first drawn with pencil,
overdrawn with pen and India ink, and painted with Winsor & Newton water color and gouache,
on Oram and Robinson water color boards.
Printed in Hong Kong
2 4 6 8 10 9 7 5 3 1
Library of Congress Cataloging-in-Publication Data
Goble, Paul.
Storm Maker's tipi / story and illustrations by Paul Goble.—1st ed.
p.   cm.
"A Richard Jackson book"
ISBN 0-689-84137-X
1. Tipis—Juvenile literature. 2. Siksika Indians—Dwellings—Juvenile literature. 3. Siksika Indians—Folklore. [1. Tipis—Folklore. 2. Siksika
Indians—Folklore. 3. Indians of North America—Great Plains—Folklore. 4. Folklore—Great Plains.] I. Title.
E99.S54 G64 2001
398.2'089'973—dc21   00-040154

for

Ben, Katie, and Tom Goble
Samuel, Anna, and Rachel Hor

This story is based on a Blackfoot legend told in *The Old North Trail* by Walter McClintock,
Macmillan, London, 1910, and also in *Painted Tipis and Picture-writing of the Blackfeet Indians,*
Southwest Museum Leaflet #6, Los Angeles, 1936.
A similar legend is told by George Bird Grinnell in *The Lodges of the Blackfeet,*
American Anthropologist, Vol. 3, G. P. Putnam's Sons, New York, 1901.
This particular lodge, known as Storm Maker's or the Snow Tipi,
has not been a part of Blackfoot tipi circles since the early 1900s.
Anyone who wants to know more about tipis should read *The Indian Tipi,*
by Reginald and Gladys Laubin, University of Oklahoma Press, Norman, 1957.
Thank you Larry Belitz and Ken Woody for your help with buffalo skin tipi covers.
Thank you my beloved wife, Janet.

Storm Maker's Tipi

story and illustrations by
PAUL GOBLE

A Richard Jackson Book
Atheneum Books for Young Readers
New York London Toronto Sydney Singapore

**In
the
beginning,**
when the Great Spirit
had made the first man and woman,
he told Napi who was his helper:
"Stay close to Man and Woman
and look after all their needs."
Man and Woman had no shelter at that time,
but when Storm Maker blew the first winds of winter,
they shivered, huddling close to their cooking fire.
Napi knew they would need a shelter.
While he was thinking about it,
a yellow leaf from a cottonwood tree blew onto his head.
"Yes!" he thought.
"This leaf has the shape of a good shelter!"

*Look at a cottonwood leaf;
you will see it is shaped like Napi's tipi.*

Napi looked about him
and gathered everything he needed.
He shaped them to make a tipi
for Man and Woman.

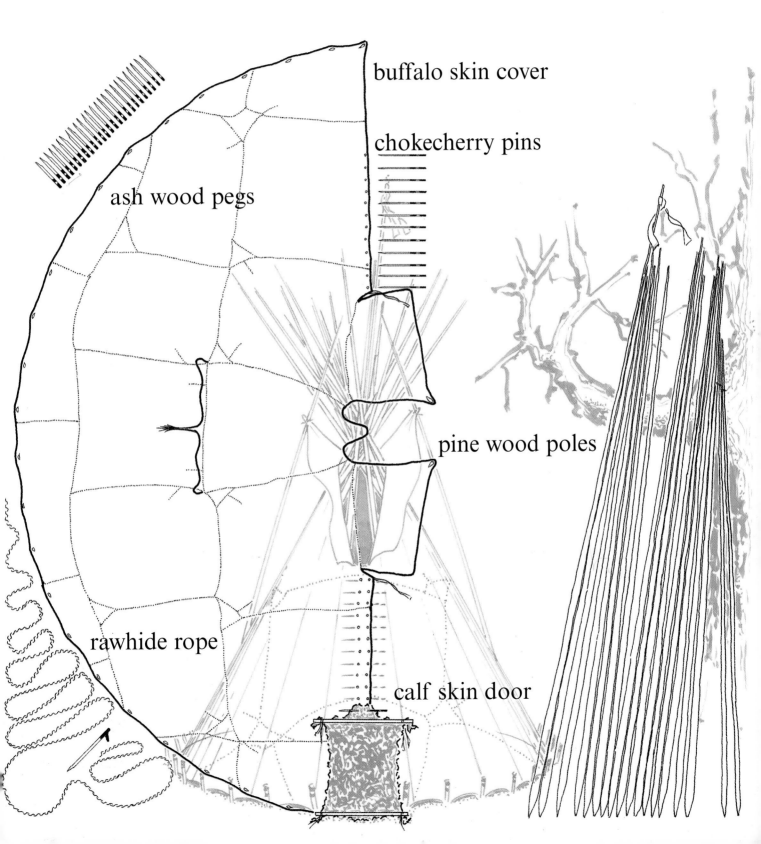

buffalo skin cover

chokecherry pins

ash wood pegs

pine wood poles

rawhide rope

calf skin door

Napi taught Man and Woman
how to pitch their tipi.

Lay the tipi cover on the ground with straight side on an east/west axis.

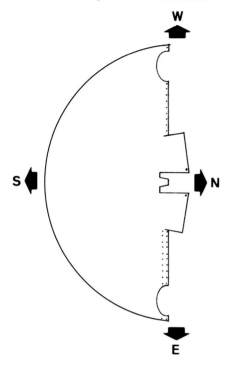

Place two poles on a north/south axis, with their butts projecting slightly from the edge of the cover.
Place two more poles about 2/3 the distance between south and east.

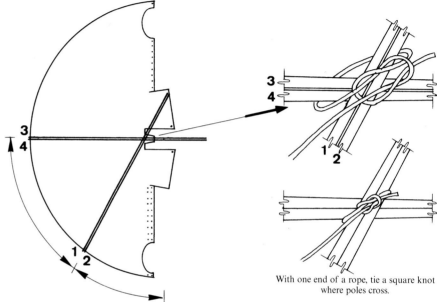

With one end of a rope, tie a square knot where poles cross.

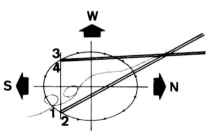

Keeping poles in the same alignment, lift them off the cover and put them down where the tipi is to be pitched.

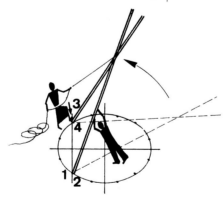

Raise the four poles, pulling on the rope.

Leave poles #1 and #3 in place.
Spread poles #2 and #4.
This tightens the square knot and forms a foundation of four poles.

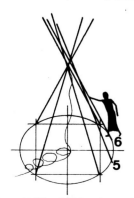

Place poles #5 and #6 into the crotch of foundation poles.

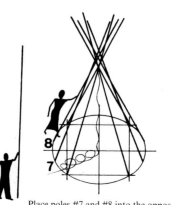

Place poles #7 and #8 into the opposite crotch.

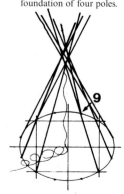

Place pole #9.

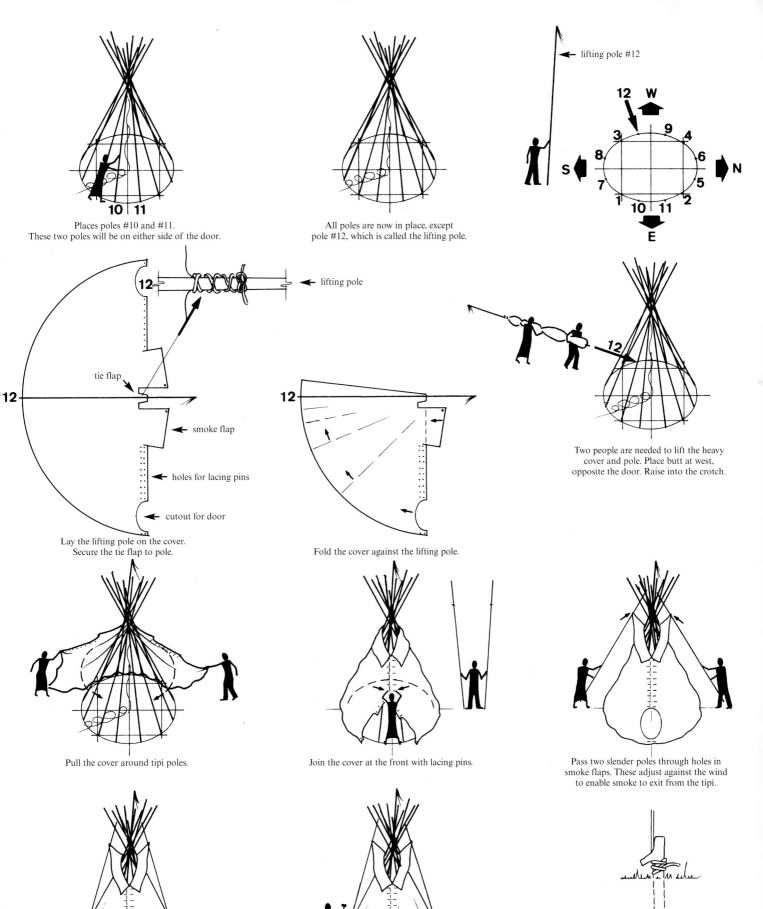

Places poles #10 and #11.
These two poles will be on either side of the door.

All poles are now in place, except
pole #12, which is called the lifting pole.

lifting pole #12

12 W
3   9   4
8   6
7   5
S   N
1   10 11 2
E

lifting pole

tie flap

smoke flap

holes for lacing pins

cutout for door

Lay the lifting pole on the cover.
Secure the tie flap to pole.

Fold the cover against the lifting pole.

Two people are needed to lift the heavy
cover and pole. Place butt at west,
opposite the door. Raise into the crotch.

Pull the cover around tipi poles.

Join the cover at the front with lacing pins.

Pass two slender poles through holes in
smoke flaps. These adjust against the wind
to enable smoke to exit from the tipi.

From inside, push poles outward to tighten
cover.

Hammer in pegs around the bottom.

Hammer in an anchor peg, inside where
the rope hangs down from the crotch, and tie it.

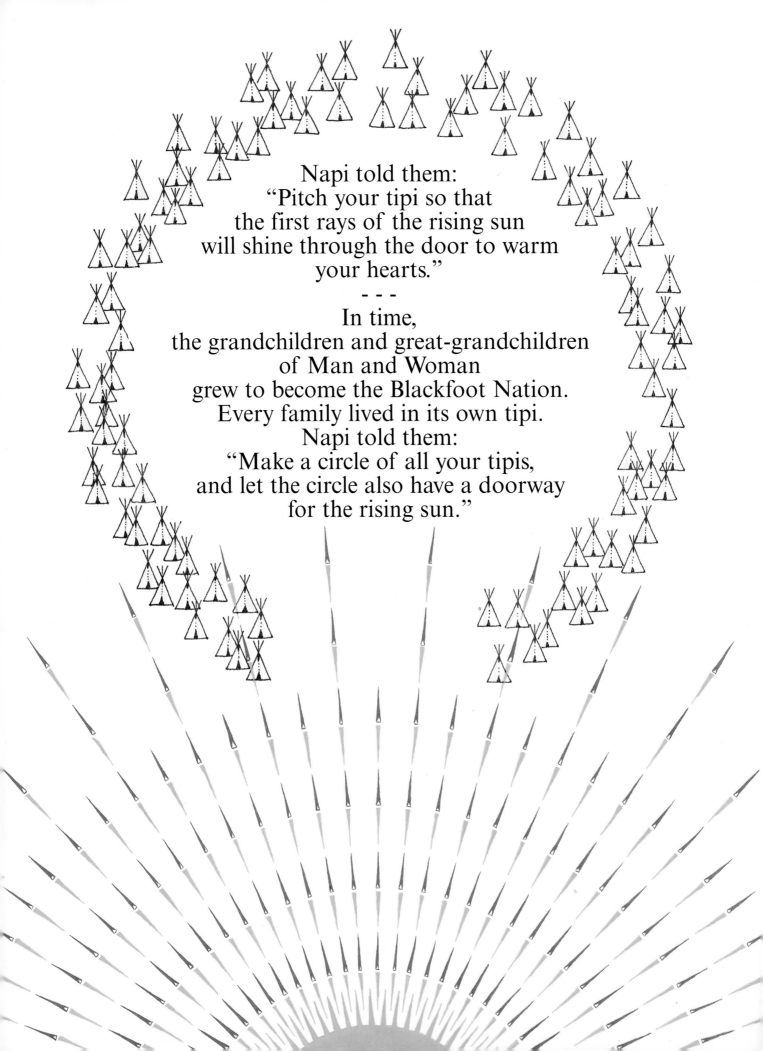

Napi told them:
"Pitch your tipi so that
the first rays of the rising sun
will shine through the door to warm
your hearts."

- - -

In time,
the grandchildren and great-grandchildren
of Man and Woman
grew to become the Blackfoot Nation.
Every family lived in its own tipi.
Napi told them:
"Make a circle of all your tipis,
and let the circle also have a doorway
for the rising sun."

Napi gave the people horses
to carry their tipis and belongings so they could
follow the wandering herds of buffalo.

Then Napi told them:
"I have given you tipis to protect you,
but shade and warmth are not enough
without the Great Spirit's blessing.
He may send
Buffalo or Otter, Bear or Snake, Rock or Crow
to help you.
Learn to hear what the spirits say!"

*This is a story about a hunter who was saved
by Storm Maker, the Bad Weather spirit,
and was given designs to paint on his tipi
to protect him.*

ONE DAY A MAN CALLED SACRED OTTER
and his son, Morning Plume, saddled their horses
and rode away from the tipi camp.
In those days Sacred Otter was a leader
of his Blackfoot people.
Morning Plume was old enough to hunt,
and his father was teaching him.

It was a glorious morning.
The trees had dropped their leaves,
but Storm Maker, Bringer of Blizzards,
still seemed to be asleep.

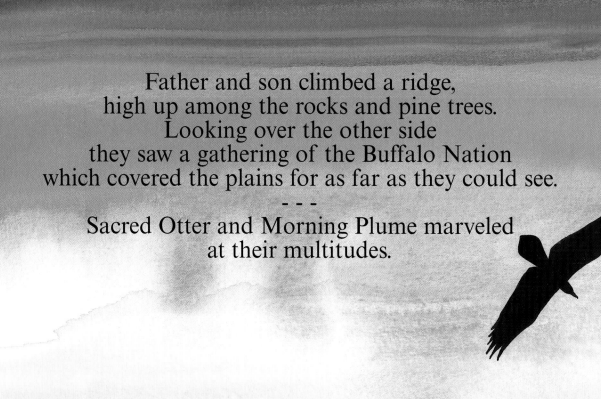

Father and son climbed a ridge,
high up among the rocks and pine trees.
Looking over the other side
they saw a gathering of the Buffalo Nation
which covered the plains for as far as they could see.
- - -
Sacred Otter and Morning Plume marveled
at their multitudes.

They rode down from the ridge.
As they came closer,
the buffaloes at the edge of the throng started to run.
Soon they were all running and the rumble of hooves
became thunder which shook the ground.

Sacred Otter led at a gallop through clouds of dust,
right among the huge shaggy animals.
Following his father's example, Morning Plume rode
up behind a buffalo,
and when alongside pulled his arrow back on the
bowstring to its full length, and let it go.

Morning Plume had killed his first buffalo.
He was learning to feed his people.
But while they were skinning the animal,
they never noticed Storm Maker approaching.
Out of the murky northern horizon white snow clouds
were rushing across the plains.
When they saw Bringer of Blizzards,
he was sweeping down upon them!
- - -
Blinded by the wind-driven snow, they cowered behind
the shelter of the dead buffalo.
Sacred Otter lay close to his son
and pulled the fresh skin over them.
Snow drifted. The skin froze.
They were protected from the terrible cold and wind.

In the darkness underneath the snow,
Sacred Otter did not know night from day.
He hardly knew whether he was awake or sleeping.
Perhaps he was dreaming?

- - -

*Then he was walking again,
through a thicket of bushes.
He could see a tipi in the distance.
He wanted to reach it, but wondered if he would
ever be able to. He shivered.
Wrapping his blanket tighter around him,
Sacred Otter walked on.*

The tipi was immense, like no other he had seen. Its yellow top and red winter sun reached the sky, and stretching down from it were the legs and claws of the fearsome Thunder Bird who lives in the storm clouds.

Sacred Otter walked cautiously around to the front, wondering who lived in such a tipi. There was a red buffalo head with green eyes, and bunches of horsehair were hanging beside the door. This was closed, yet wisps of smoke wafting through the smoke hole above told Sacred Otter that somebody was inside. . . .

"I know you are standing out there!"
a big voice from inside said.
"Why don't you come in?"

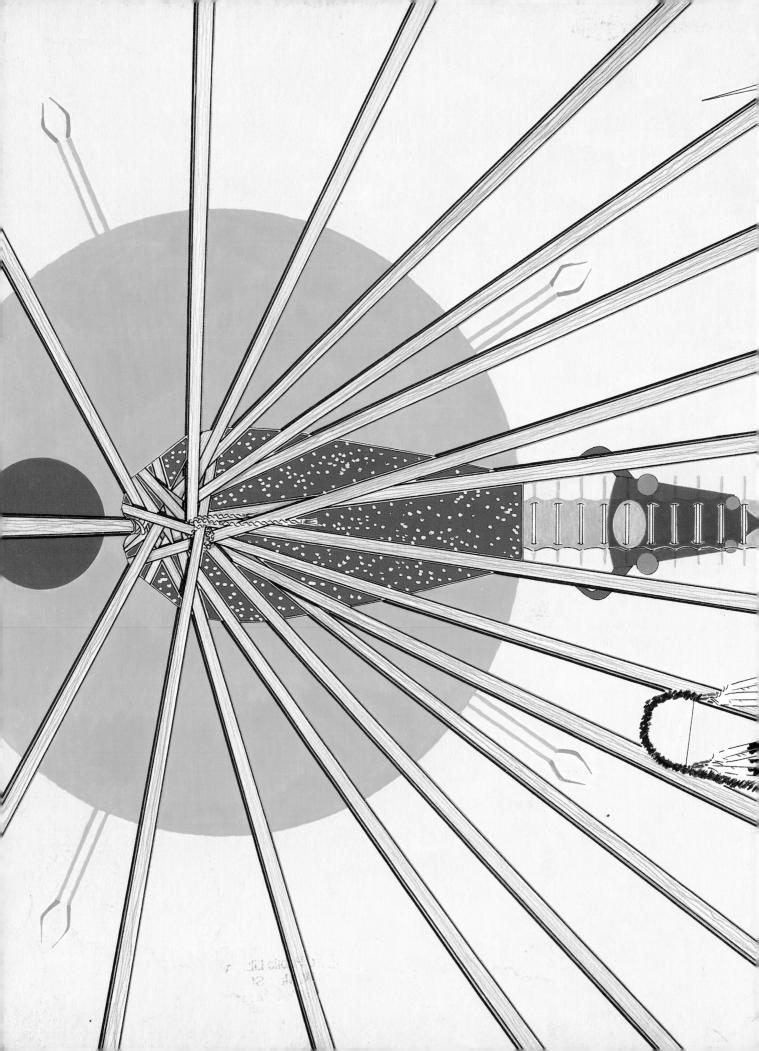

Sacred Otter stepped inside the enormous tipi.
An old man was sitting at the back, smoking his pipe.
"I am Storm Maker, Bringer of Blizzards," he said at last.
"Everyone fears me! You know my power!
But I will not let you and your boy die in this storm.
I have brought you here to show you my tipi.
When the warm weather returns, paint one just like it.
Then your family will be safe from storms always.
Hang bunches of horsehair by your door
and you will be rich with many horses as well!"

– – –

Sacred Otter awoke
and saw the snows and winds had abated.

Storm Maker kept his promise and held back the blizzard
until Sacred Otter reached home again with his son.
- - -
When springtime came,
people helped paint Storm Maker's tipi,
exactly as Sacred Otter remembered it.
They tied bunches of horsehair by the door.
They called it the Snow Tipi, or the Bad Weather Lodge.

It is remembered that Sacred Otter once saved
his people. It happened this way:
All powerful Storm Maker approached,
threatening to destroy the tipis and kill everyone.
Holding up his pipe, Sacred Otter walked away from
the camp to meet the swirling clouds and lightning.
"Storm Maker!" he called. "Hear me!
Pity the women and children, as you once pitied my
youngest son! Turn aside! We want to live!"
Storm Maker heard him.
The wind died, and in the dark stillness
the terrible storm passed around them.

The bunches of horsehair hanging by his door
brought Sacred Otter good luck,
as Storm Maker had said they would!
Legend tells that Sacred Otter was not only brave
in capturing many horses from the enemy,
but that he was also brave in generosity,
by giving them all away!

It is good to remember the days when men and
women better understood the spirits.
What Napi foretold came true:
Bear and Eagle, Fish and Tree, Horse and Beaver,
and many others spoke and gave their tipis
so people would be safe.

Some of those old painted tipis are still pitched in
Blackfoot summer camps in Montana and Alberta.
Like Storm Maker's tipi,
each has a story of its gift by the spirits.
These remind us that if we listen,
we, too, can learn whatever we most need to know.

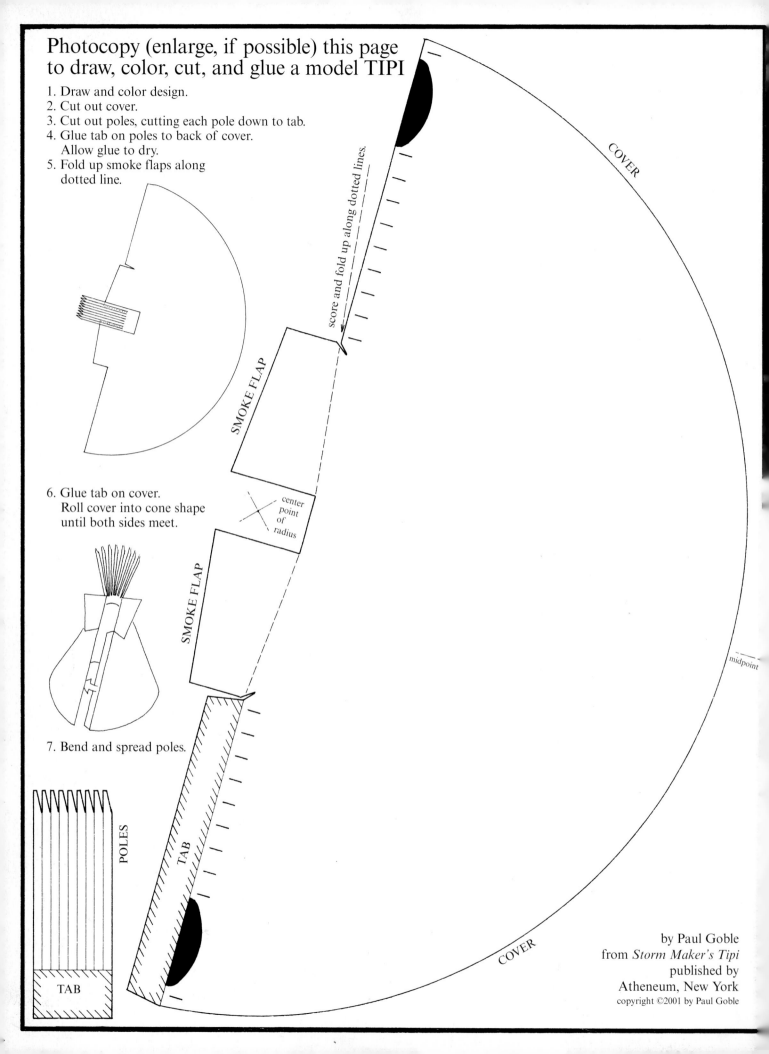

Photocopy (enlarge, if possible) this page to draw, color, cut, and glue a model TIPI

1. Draw and color design.
2. Cut out cover.
3. Cut out poles, cutting each pole down to tab.
4. Glue tab on poles to back of cover.
   Allow glue to dry.
5. Fold up smoke flaps along
   dotted line.

6. Glue tab on cover.
   Roll cover into cone shape
   until both sides meet.

7. Bend and spread poles.

COVER

score and fold up along dotted lines.

SMOKE FLAP

center
point
of
radius

SMOKE FLAP

midpoint

POLES

TAB

TAB

COVER

by Paul Goble
from *Storm Maker's Tipi*
published by
Atheneum, New York

Now set up the tipi.
Around the bottom
Drive in the pegs!
Drive in the pegs!
In the meantime I shall cook.
Lakota

That wind!
That wind!
Shakes my tipi!
Shakes my tipi!
And sings a song for me.
Kiowa

sunrise
through
the
smoke
hole

DISCARD